When I Was Five

by Arthur Howard

Harcourt Brace and Company

San Diego   New York   London

Library of Congress Cataloging-in-Publication Data
Howard, Arthur.
When I was five/Arthur Howard.—1st ed.
p.   cm.
Summary: A six-year-old boy describes the things he liked
when he was five and compares them to the things he likes now.
ISBN 0-15-200261-8
[1. Growth—Fiction. 2. Identity—Fiction. 3. Friendship—Fiction.]
I. Title.
PZ7.H8324Wh   1996
[E]—dc20   94-43987

First edition   A B C D E

Printed in Singapore

for Beverly

When I was five

or a cowboy

or both.

When I
was five
this was
my favorite
kind of
car,

this was
my favorite
kind of dinosaur,

and this was my
best friend, Mark.

Mark
had
a
dog
named
Peggy,

a brother who used bad words,

and bunk beds—
my favorite
kind of bed
when I was five.

Now I'm six

and I want to be a

major-league baseball player

or a deep-sea diver.

Now that I'm six

this is my favorite kind of car,

this is my favorite
kind of dinosaur,

this is my second-best hiding place

(my favorite one is a secret),

and this is my best friend, Mark.

Some things never change.

The illustrations in this book were done in watercolor,

gouache, and black pencil on 90 lb. drawing paper.

The text was hand-lettered by Arthur Howard.

Color separations by Bright Arts, Ltd., Singapore

Printed and bound by Tien Wah Press, Singapore

This book was printed with soya-based inks on Leykam

recycled paper, which contains more than 20 percent postconsumer

waste and has a total recycled content of at least 50 percent.

Production supervision by Warren Wallerstein and Diana Ford

Designed by Arthur Howard and Camilla Filancia